**BALLPARK Mysteries 10**

# THE ROOKIE
# BLUE JAY

#1 *The Fenway Foul-Up*

#2 *The Pinstripe Ghost*

#3 *The L.A. Dodger*

#4 *The Astro Outlaw*

#5 *The All-Star Joker*

#6 *The Wrigley Riddle*

#7 *The San Francisco Splash*

#8 *The Missing Marlin*

#9 *The Philly Fake*

#10 *The Rookie Blue Jay*

#11 *The Tiger Troubles*

**Also by David A. Kelly**

*Babe Ruth and the Baseball Curse*

# THE ROOKIE
# BLUE JAY

by David A. Kelly

illustrated by Mark Meyers

A STEPPING STONE BOOK™

Random House 🏠 New York

*This book is dedicated to my father, Kevin Kelly,*
*who sneaked me into a hotel restaurant when I was ten to meet*
*Hank Aaron and get his autograph. —D.A.K.*

*To the Garvonsons. —M.M.*

*"If my uniform doesn't get dirty, I haven't done anything in*
*the baseball game." —Ricky Henderson, outfielder on the 1993*
*Toronto Blue Jays team, which won the World Series*

Text copyright © 2015 by David A. Kelly
Cover art and interior illustrations copyright © 2015 by Mark Meyers

All rights reserved. Published in the United States by Random House Children's Books, a division of Random House LLC, a Penguin Random House Company, New York.

Random House and the colophon are registered trademarks and A Stepping Stone Book and the colophon are trademarks of Random House LLC. Ballpark Mysteries® is a registered trademark of Upside Research, Inc.

Visit us on the Web!
SteppingStonesBooks.com
randomhouse.com/kids
Educators and librarians, for a variety of teaching tools, visit us at
RHTeachersLibrarians.com

*Library of Congress Cataloging-in-Publication Data*
Kelly, David A.
The rookie Blue Jay / by David A. Kelly ; illustrated by Mark Meyers.
pages cm. — (Ballpark mysteries ; 10)
"A Stepping Stone book."
Summary: While staying at a hotel built as part of the Toronto Blue Jays' baseball stadium, where guests can watch games from their room, cousins Mike and Kate spot strange blue lights flashing across the bull pen and decide to investigate.
ISBN 978-0-385-37875-8 (pbk.) — ISBN 978-0-385-37876-5 (lib. bdg.) —
ISBN 978-0-385-37877-2 (ebook)
[1. Baseball—Fiction. 2. Toronto Blue Jays (Baseball team)—Fiction. 3. Cousins—Fiction. 4. Toronto (Ont.)—Fiction. 5. Canada—Fiction. 6. Mystery and detective stories.]
I. Meyers, Mark, illustrator. II. Title. PZ7.K2936Ro 2015   [Fic] — dc23   2013045713

Printed in the United States of America
10 9 8 7 6 5 4 3 2 1

This book has been officially leveled by using the
F&P Text Level Gradient™ Leveling System.

Random House Children's Books supports the First Amendment
and celebrates the right to read.

# Contents

Chapter 1    **Over the Falls**                    1

Chapter 2    **A Hotel Mystery**                   9

Chapter 3    **Midnight Lights**                  16

Chapter 4    **Trouble Sleeping**                 25

Chapter 5    **A Surprise Find**                  36

Chapter 6    **The Streak**                       43

Chapter 7    **The Glowing Light**                51

Chapter 8    **Slap Shot**                        59

Chapter 9    **Time Travel**                      71

Chapter 10   **A Confession**                     80

Chapter 11   **Rookie of the Year**               86

**Dugout Notes ☆**
**Toronto Blue Jays Ballpark**                    99

# Over the Falls

Mike Walsh grabbed the railing at the front of the sightseeing boat. The boat surged against a strong current, and a spray of water shot up and drenched his blue poncho. Mike took a deep breath. Then he yelled as loudly as he could, "MIKE WALSH IS THE BEST BASEBALL PLAYER EVERRRRRRRR!"

Lots of people stood near Mike, but no one noticed. They were too busy snapping pictures of Niagara Falls. Millions of gallons of water crashed down with a thundering roar in front of the boat. Clouds of mist rose up from the base of the falls.

Mike's cousin Kate Hopkins leaned in close to him. "I DON'T THINK THEY CAN HEAR YOU!" she yelled. "THE FALLS ARE TOO LOUD!"

Mike, Kate, and Kate's mother were taking a ride on the *Maid of the Mist,* a boat that took tourists to the bottom of one of the largest waterfalls in the world.

Mrs. Hopkins worked as a sports reporter. She often took Kate and Mike with her to baseball stadiums. They had stopped to see Niagara Falls on their way from Cooperstown, New York, to Toronto, Canada. In Toronto, they were going to go to a Blue Jays baseball game. Just after lunch, they had crossed the border into Canada.

Up close, the rumble of the waterfall was so

loud that Mike and Kate stopped trying to talk. Instead, they watched the flood of water crash down in front of them. After the boat cruised close to the base of the falls, it headed back downstream.

As the noise of the falls died away, Mike and Kate slipped off their dripping ponchos. Mike put on his brand-new blue and white Toronto Blue Jays baseball cap. He had bought it at a shop before they boarded the boat.

Kate tossed her long brown hair to fling off drops of water. "Wow, that was cool!" she said.

"It sure was," Mike said as he tightened his cap. "And just think, my mom gets mad when I leave the water running while I brush my teeth!"

Mrs. Hopkins smiled. "How about I take a picture of you with the falls in the background?" she asked. "You can show it to your mother next time you leave the water on."

Mike and Kate stood against the boat's railing while Mrs. Hopkins took a picture. A few minutes later, the boat docked. After they got off, Kate, Mike, and Mrs. Hopkins caught a trolley back to the welcome center at the top of the falls.

Outside the welcome center stood a tall red, white, and blue barrel. Nearby was a large, round metal tank and a bunch of black inner tubes roped together. They were part of a Niagara Falls exhibit that showed different things people had used to ride over the falls.

"Those inner tubes don't look safe," Mike said. "I'd take them down a hill in the winter, but definitely *not* over those falls!"

Kate studied the barrel. "When I did that school report on Canada, I read a book about Niagara Falls. It said that Annie Edison Taylor was the first person to go over the falls in a barrel and live," Kate said. She was always reading. "She did it on her sixty-third birthday in 1901."

"Now that's a birthday present!" Mike said. "I was thinking of going on a roller coaster for my birthday. Maybe I should try that instead!"

"I don't think your mom would like that," Kate's mother said. "But these falls do attract daredevils. Just a few years ago, a man walked across them on a tightrope!"

Behind the exhibit, a sidewalk ran next to the river above the falls. Nearby was a white tent with open sides. Inside three men sat behind a long table. A line of kids waited to get in.

"Hey, Aunt Laura, can we go check that out?" Mike asked.

"Sure," Mrs. Hopkins said. "Stay together,

and I'll meet you by the falls in a few minutes."

Mike and Kate ran over to the tent. The sign next to it read HOCKEY AT THE FALLS. MEET A HALL OF FAME HOCKEY PLAYER!

"Neat!" Mike said. He pointed to his hat. "Maybe I can get one of them to sign my new Blue Jays hat."

Kate shook her head. "These are *hockey* players, not baseball players, Mike," she said. "Remember, we're in Canada now. They're crazy for hockey here."

"That's all right," Mike said. He leaned over and pretended to hit a hockey puck with an imaginary stick. "I like all sports, especially ones where you can score!"

Mike and Kate lined up behind the other kids. It only took five minutes to go through the tent. Mike and Kate met the players and came out holding hockey pucks. Both were signed in

bright silver marker. When Mike spotted Kate's mom at the railing near the river, they ran over to show her.

Mrs. Hopkins studied the signed hockey pucks. "Very nice!" she said. "Maybe we can get some signed baseballs at the Blue Jays game. Then we'll have something from America's *and* Canada's favorite sports!"

They leaned over the railing to get a better look at the river rushing by. The water seemed to speed up as it got closer to the falls.

A swirling gust of wind blew by. It whooshed past Kate's hair, swirling it all around her face. It swept by Mike and lifted the brim of his Blue Jays baseball cap.

"Hey, my hat!" Mike yelled. The wind had blown it right off! It fluttered end over end, then landed in the rushing Niagara River.

His baseball cap was headed straight for the falls!

# A Hotel Mystery

Just twenty feet downstream, the water poured over the lip of Niagara Falls and crashed to the rocks at the bottom. Mike ran along the edge until he found another open spot at the railing. The hat was swirling along the shoreline. He leaned over to grab the hat when it went by, but Kate's mother pulled him back.

"That's not safe," she said. "I don't want *you* falling in, too!"

"I could have had it!" Mike said. The hat was directly in front of him.

Suddenly, a bald man stepped up to the railing next to Mike. He swooped the blade of a hockey stick underwater. In one quick motion, he snagged Mike's hat and saved it from the falls!

The hat dangled at the end of the stick. When it was safely over the railing, the man grabbed the dripping hat.

"Wow, thanks!" Mike cried. "That's what I call a hat trick!"

The man took off his sunglasses. He had deep blue eyes and bushy eyebrows. He wore a white and blue hockey jersey with a maple leaf on the front. Mike recognized him—he was one of the hockey players from the tent.

The man tossed the Blue Jays cap to Mike. "You're lucky," he said. "I almost didn't rescue it because it's a baseball hat. The only sport that really matters around here is hockey!"

"Thanks for saving it," Mike said. "You're one of the Hall of Fame hockey players, right?"

"That's right," the man said. "I'm Buck.

Used to play for the Toronto Maple Leafs." Buck pointed at Mike's hat. "You like baseball?"

"Yup," Mike said. "It's my favorite sport."

Buck let out a big sigh. "You sound like my son. Always loved baseball more than hockey," he said. "The Blue Jays are a good team, but if you ask me, hockey's the real deal." Buck gave Mike a nod and walked back to the tent.

Mike, Kate, and Mrs. Hopkins headed off to explore the town. It was filled with fun things to do. Mike and Kate had never seen so many T-shirt shops, fudge stores, and arcades. At the end of the street they went into a museum of oddities. Inside were lots of strange exhibits, including mummies, a stuffed dog with extra feet, and pictures of super-tall people.

They made it back to the car just as it was getting dark. Their hotel in Toronto was an hour and a half away.

"I forgot to tell you that there's something special about our hotel," Mrs. Hopkins said when they reached the highway.

"Is it really tall?" Mike asked.

"Does it have a water park in it?" Kate asked.

"Maybe it has an ice cream sundae bar in every room!" Mike said.

"Or how about a batting cage?" Kate put in.

Mrs. Hopkins laughed. "No, it doesn't have any of those, but Kate's batting cage guess is a good idea. Keep trying!"

Kate and Mike kept throwing out guesses as they drove. But everything they suggested, from an animal park to slides going out the windows, was wrong. When they ran out of ideas, Mrs. Hopkins played an audiobook of folk tales and ghost stories.

Mike especially liked one story about ghost

lights. According to the legend, ghost lights were spooky glowing lights that floated in the air and led people into trouble. Mike liked the story so much he made Mrs. Hopkins play it a second time. After that, Mike imagined he kept seeing ghost lights in the car's windshield, until Mrs. Hopkins finally pointed out they were just the reflections of the headlights from other cars.

By the time Mrs. Hopkins, Kate, and Mike pulled up to the door of the hotel, it was late. Mrs. Hopkins checked in at the front desk, while Mike and Kate circled around in the revolving door. When they got to the door of their room a few minutes later, Mrs. Hopkins paused. "Any last guesses as to what's special about this hotel?" she asked.

Mike grabbed an imaginary pole in front of him. "Maybe the room has two floors and there's a fire pole we can slide down to get from one to the other!" he said. "That would be cool!"

"Or hot," Kate said, "since it's a fire pole!"

Mrs. Hopkins laughed. "It would be," she said as she unlocked the door. "But that's not it. Take a look."

# Midnight Lights

Mike and Kate rushed into the room. They dropped their suitcases and scrambled around. Kate checked out the bathroom. Mike looked under the beds and in the closet. But they didn't find anything unusual.

"We give up, Mom," Kate said. "What's so special about the room?"

Kate's mother smiled. "I'll show you," she said. She led them to the window and opened the curtains.

The hotel room was inside the Toronto Blue

Jays' baseball stadium! Through the window, Mike and Kate could see the green grass of the outfield just below them. On the other side of the field, thousands of empty blue seats curved around home plate and the infield.

"You're kidding!" Mike said. "We're staying inside the ballpark?" He pressed his nose against the glass to get a better look.

"Wow!" Kate said.

"It's one of a kind," Mrs. Hopkins said. "The Blue Jays thought it would be really neat to have hotel rooms with a view of the baseball diamond, so they built this hotel as part of the stadium. You can even watch baseball games right from the room if you want!"

Mrs. Hopkins unlocked a latch on the window. The top half of the window slid wide open. Mike and Kate rested their arms on the edge and looked out into the stadium.

Mike stuck his hand through the window and waved it around. "Hey, maybe I could catch a home run up here," he said. "Or get the players to throw me a ball. If I lived here, I'd never leave!"

Kate and Mike spent the next few minutes gazing out at the stadium. The field below was set up for the next day's batting practice, with screens in front of the pitching mound and second base.

"Time for bed," Mrs. Hopkins said as she finally shooed Mike and Kate away from the window. "The ballpark will still be here tomorrow."

Mike and Kate put on their pajamas. Mike's pajamas were white with baseball bats, balls, and gloves all over them. Kate's had red stripes and a number on the back, like a uniform. Kate brushed her teeth first. Mike pretended to lose his toothbrush. But Mrs. Hopkins found it under Mike's suitcase and sent him in next.

Mrs. Hopkins rolled out a sleeping bag near the window. "There are only two beds. You'll have to decide who gets the bed and who gets the sleeping bag," she said.

"Let's flip a coin," Mike said. He pulled out a quarter from his pants pocket. Since it was a Canadian quarter, it looked different. He looked closely at the coin. One side had an image of the queen of England. The other had a picture of an animal with big antlers. "I call the moose," he said.

Kate grimaced. "It's a *caribou,* you moosehead!" she said. "But that's okay, I'll take the queen."

Kate took the quarter from Mike and flipped it into the air with her thumb. She caught it in her right hand and smacked it down on her wrist. Then she lifted her hand. The face of the quarter stared up at her.

"Heads! It's the queen," she said. "I call the bed."

Mike dropped onto the sleeping bag and crawled inside it. "I didn't want the bed, anyway," his muffled voice called out. "I'd rather sleep on the floor, since it's closer to the field."

Mrs. Hopkins turned off the light. A few minutes later, Kate and Mike were fast asleep.

★ ★ ★

Just before midnight, Mike woke up thirsty. He climbed out of his sleeping bag and got a drink of water from the bathroom sink. On his way back, he paused to sneak a look at the stadium.

Mike opened the curtains just enough so he could see out. The stadium was completely empty and dark, except for a few red EXIT signs. Mike stared at the field. It would be so cool to run around the bases of the empty stadium in the dark! Then he noticed a strange blue flicker in the Blue Jays bull pen, right below their hotel room.

At first he barely saw it. But when Mike leaned forward and pressed his face against the window, he saw it again. A blue flicker streaked from one end of the bull pen to the other!

Mike raced over to Kate's bed and shook her arm until she woke up. He put his finger to his

lips to signal that Kate should keep quiet.

"You've got to see what's happening in the bull pen," he whispered.

Mike led Kate to the window.

A streak of blue light flashed across the bull pen again.

Kate's sleepy eyes popped open. She stood on her tiptoes to get a better look. "I can't believe it," she whispered.

One streak of blue light followed the other. They zipped across the bull pen. Sometimes they'd linger at the far end and then slowly move back to the other end.

Kate nodded knowingly. "Do you know what that is?" she asked.

"No, what?" Mike asked.

"It's a ghost light!"

# Trouble Sleeping

From the floor-to-ceiling windows in the hotel restaurant the next morning, Mike and Kate scanned the stadium. But all they saw were row after row of empty blue seats and the green turf of the field.

"Hey, kids, come on back to the table. Your waffles are getting cold," Mrs. Hopkins called out. "What are you two so interested in over there?"

Kate glanced at Mike as they sat down at the table. He shrugged and then nodded.

"Ghost lights!" Kate said.

"Ghost lights?" Mrs. Hopkins said. "In the Blue Jays' stadium? What are they doing— beckoning players to the minor leagues?"

Kate laughed and took a bite of her eggs and Canadian bacon.

Mike shook his head. "No, it was really strange," he said. "I woke up in the middle of the night and looked out the window. Strange lights kept flying back and forth in the bull pen. I even woke up Kate and showed her."

Kate nodded. "It was weird," she added. "We weren't imagining things. There *was* something there!"

"Well, I can't explain the strange lights in the Blue Jays bull pen," Mrs. Hopkins said. "But I *can* introduce you to a Blue Jays player. How would you like that?"

"Really?" Kate asked. "That would be great!"

"Who is it?" Mike asked.

"Dusty, their best new player," Mrs. Hopkins said. "He just joined the team last year, and he's up for the Rookie of the Year Award. He hasn't made an error all season. I'm interviewing him after breakfast, and he said you two could come along."

"Cool!" Mike said as he poured maple syrup on his waffles. "Maybe we can ask him about the ghost lights."

After Mike, Kate, and Mrs. Hopkins finished breakfast, they paid and went outside. To get to the stadium, they had to walk around the ballpark to the main entrance. Mrs. Hopkins showed the security guard her press pass. He led them to the team's locker room and opened the door. "Dusty's expecting you," the security guard said.

The Blue Jays locker room was long and wide. It had a big ceiling that swooped up on one side. Players' lockers lined each wall. Tables, couches, and big leather chairs on wheels were arranged in the middle of the room. It was early, so there were only a few players in the locker room. One waved them over.

"Hello! I'm Dusty," he said as he stood up to shake hands. Dusty was tall with curly hair. He looked much younger than most of the baseball players Mike and Kate had met before.

Mike whistled. "Wow, what a cool clubhouse," he said.

"It is nice," Dusty said. "The team wanted to make it feel like home." He glanced around the room and let out a long sigh. "I'll miss it when I leave."

Dusty picked up a baseball off a table and rolled it back and forth between his hands. He turned to Mrs. Hopkins. "I guess you want to interview me?" he said.

Mrs. Hopkins took out a pad of paper to take notes. "Yes, thanks. You haven't made an error all season long, and you've had a hit in each of the last fifteen games," she said. "How are you keeping that streak alive?"

Dusty brightened up a bit. He smiled a toothy grin. "Well, I always wear my lucky T-shirt for games," he said. He pointed at the shirt he was wearing. It had a white maple leaf on the front, and the deep blue of the shirt matched his eyes.

Mrs. Hopkins wrote down Dusty's answer. Then she flipped through her notes. "I have a bunch of questions," she said. "Can Mike and Kate wait somewhere while I interview you?"

Dusty shrugged. "Sure," he said. He pointed across the room to a locker. It had the name DUSTY MARTIN printed above it. "Why don't you two sit down there?"

Mike and Kate walked over and plopped down on the chairs in front of Dusty's locker. Inside hung bright blue game jerseys. Pairs of cleats lined the bottom. A few baseballs rested on a shelf, along with a tan and black glove. The sides of the locker were filled with pictures of Dusty. There were lots of him from when he was younger, playing baseball and hockey. In one picture, he was standing on skates on an ice rink with a hockey stick and a trophy.

When Mrs. Hopkins was done, she called Mike and Kate back. Dusty had excused himself to get a cup of coffee.

When he returned, he slumped down in his chair and took a big sip of coffee. He seemed lost in thought. He shook his head as if he were trying to get cobwebs out.

After a minute, Mrs. Hopkins broke the silence. "Are you okay, Dusty?" she asked.

Dusty nodded slowly. "Sorry," he said. "I'm tired. I've been having a little trouble sleeping lately. I almost made my first error of the season a few days ago because I was so tired."

Mike jumped out of his seat. "I've been having trouble sleeping, too!" he said. "Last night I woke up at midnight and saw something really strange in the stadium."

Dusty suddenly sat up straight. "What do you mean?" he asked. "Did you see someone?"

"No," Kate said. "We saw these weird glowing lights from our hotel window."

Mike hopped from side to side. "The blue lights streaked from one side of the bull pen to the other, like this," he said as he hopped. "Then, all of a sudden, they stopped!"

Dusty fidgeted with his coffee cup. "That's odd," he said.

"We think they're ghost lights," Kate said. "We listened to an audiobook in the car that said ghost lights lead people into trouble."

Mike made a slashing motion across his neck and fell to the floor as if he were dead. "Sometimes they even lure you to your death," he said from the floor.

"I don't know if they do *that*," Kate said. She pulled Mike off the floor. "Have you ever seen them, Dusty?"

"Me?" Dusty asked. He glanced down at the floor and scratched the back of his neck for a moment. "I've never—I've never seen anything in the stadium that I can't explain."

Dusty checked his watch and stood up. "I'm afraid I've got to get going now," he said. He led them to the clubhouse door and opened it.

"Thanks for talking with us," Mrs. Hopkins said. "Good luck with your streak. We'll be rooting for you."

"Thanks," Dusty said. He nodded at Mike and Kate. "I'll keep my eyes open for those lights. Let me know if you see them again. If I'm not in the dugout, just ask one of the workers to find me."

The door closed behind them. Mike, Kate,

and Mrs. Hopkins headed for the exit.

"Was he nervous or something when we asked about the ghost lights?" Kate asked as they walked outside. "He seemed to want to get rid of us in a hurry."

"Oh, I don't know," Mrs. Hopkins said. "He said he was having trouble sleeping. He's probably just stressed about the streak."

"I don't think that's why he's tired," Mike said.

"You don't?" Kate asked. "Why's he tired, then?"

"I think he's having trouble sleeping because he must have seen the lights, too!"

# A Surprise Find

"Nice hit!" Kate shouted as a ball sailed high into the outfield. A group of Blue Jays players chased the baseball until one called it and it dropped into his glove. The player tossed the ball to a batboy standing behind a big protective screen near second base.

Mike, Kate, and Mrs. Hopkins had just come back from an early lunch to watch batting practice. The Blue Jays were playing the New York Mets in an afternoon game. On the field, the players were busy practicing. Near home plate, a coach threw balls to batters. Each batter got about twenty pitches. Some batters hit towering home runs. Others hit grounders.

Kate and Mike stood by the infield fence. They watched the first few players hit. Kate's mom was on the field with other reporters. She was doing pregame interviews.

The third Blue Jays batter stepped up to the plate. He popped a foul ball that headed right for Mike and Kate.

"I've got it!" Mike called. He stretched over the fence to catch the ball. But as he leaned forward, his baseball cap slipped off his head. It fell to the ground just as the ball hit the fence and bounced back into the infield.

"Hey, my hat!" Mike said. He tried to reach for it, but his arms weren't long enough.

Next to Mike, a tall man watching batting practice leaned over and scooped the hat

up. He turned to hand it to Mike, but stopped
suddenly.

The man smiled. "Not you *again,*" he said.
It was Buck, the hockey player from Niagara

Falls. Buck handed Mike his hat.

Mike's freckled face blushed. "Sorry, I guess I was leaning over too far," he said. He slipped his hat back on. Then he pulled it down tight. "Thanks for saving my hat—again."

Buck laughed. "No problem," he said. "I usually only save hockey hats. But if you have to wear a baseball hat, at least you've got the right team."

"I thought you didn't like baseball," Kate said.

"Well, hockey's better, but my son plays baseball," Buck said. "I always wanted him to play hockey like me, but he had other ideas. And he's a lot better at baseball than I ever was at hockey."

Just then, Buck's cell phone rang. He pulled it out of his pocket. "Excuse me," he said. "I've got to take this." Buck stepped away from the fence. He walked up the steps and sat in the aisle seat of the last row.

Mike and Kate waited a few minutes for him to finish his call. But it didn't look as if Buck was going to get off his phone anytime soon. Out on the field, a new batter stepped up to the plate. Kate's mom was still interviewing a team official near the dugout.

"Want to check out the bull pen?" Kate asked. "Maybe we can find the ghost light."

Mike and Kate snaked their way through the rows of seats to the left-field corner. About twenty feet below them was the Blue Jays bull pen. It was sandwiched between the outfield and the outfield seats. A pitcher was already warming up. He threw one baseball after another to a catcher crouching at the far end. *Whiz—pop. Whiz—pop.*

Except for the catcher and pitcher, the bull

pen was empty. There were baseballs on one side and a screen behind the catcher.

"I don't see anything unusual," Kate said. "It looks like a bull pen."

"But there was something here last night," Mike said. He took off his hat and looked up to his left, near the scoreboard. "That's our room," he said. "We definitely saw something."

Kate nodded. "Well, let's look for clues," she said. "I'll do this row. You take the next one."

They split up and checked under each seat. It didn't take long for Mike to make a find.

"Hey, look at what I got!" he said. Mike held up a half-empty bottle of red PowerPunch. "I'm thirsty. Should I finish it?"

Kate wrinkled her nose. "Ew. That's gross," she said. "Keep looking. If the PowerPunch had been glowing last night, it would have been a *red* light."

Mike placed the bottle at the end of the row and continued searching. Kate finished her row. She started again a couple of rows below Mike. She didn't find anything until she got to the last seat. Kate spied something between the seat and the wall. It took a minute for her to wiggle it out.

"Mike!" Kate called. "Look what I found!"

# The Streak

Mike jumped over the seats. Kate held up a bright blue disk about the size of a doughnut. Its top and bottom were smooth, but the side was a little rough. Kate handed it to Mike.

"It's a hockey puck!" he said. He turned it over in his hands. "Cool! Someone must have left it behind."

Kate nodded. "Yeah," she said. "Remember how they gave out those American flags when we went to a Phillies game? Maybe around here they give out hockey pucks!"

Mike tossed the puck back to Kate. "My dad's got some old hockey sticks at the store," he said. Mike's father owned a sporting-goods store in Cooperstown. "Maybe we can try this out when we get home."

"Good idea," Kate said. She slipped the puck into her pocket.

They searched the rest of the seats but didn't find anything else.

Mike flipped up the last seat. It was empty underneath. "This was a bust," he said. "It's getting close to game time. At least maybe the game will be good."

Mike and Kate made it back to their seats just as "The Star-Spangled Banner" began. When it was over, Mike started to sit down, but Kate tapped him with her foot. "Pssst . . . ," she whispered. "You've got to keep standing for Canada's national anthem!"

The words of "O Canada" rang out through the ballpark. Mike stood back up as it played.

The fans all around Mike and Kate sang loudly during the last two lines of the song:

> *O Canada, we stand on guard for thee.*
> *O Canada, we stand on guard for thee.*

"Play ball!" yelled a fan with a deep voice

next to Mike and Kate. Everyone cheered wildly as the Blue Jays trotted onto the field. Dusty took his spot at second base. Mike and Kate waved to him, but he was too busy setting up for the game to notice.

The Mets' Alvin Shay led off with a strong double to right field. When he stole third base, it looked as if he might score, but Cody Clemens, the Blue Jays pitcher, shut down the next three batters for three outs.

Neither team scored in the next two innings. In the bottom of the fourth, Dusty helped the Blue Jays get their first run. He hit a single that knocked in a man on third. That put the Blue Jays ahead 1–0.

The fifth inning was tough for the Jays. Cody Clemens gave up two singles with no outs. The next batter hit a hard grounder right to Dusty, who fielded it and threw to first for the out. Even though it wasn't a hard play, Dusty's throw was high. The first baseman barely snagged it by stretching really far. If he'd missed, at least one run would have scored and Dusty would have been charged with an error.

"That was close!" Mike said. "Dusty almost broke his streak!"

Luckily, the Blue Jays got two more outs, leaving them ahead. At the end of the fifth inning, Mike and Kate were about to get up to grab some food when the Blue Jays grounds crew raced in from the outfield.

Kate grabbed Mike's elbow. "Oh! Let's watch this," she said. "I read in the program that this is the world's fastest grounds crew."

"What do you mean?" Mike asked.

Kate pointed to the field. "Most teams have wide dirt paths between the bases," she said.

"But the Blue Jays have grass between the bases. There are only small patches of dirt around the bases for sliding. That means the grounds crew doesn't have as much to do, so they finish a lot faster."

The Blue Jays grounds crew raced in at top speed from the outfield. Three people charged each base with rakes and a fresh base. In seconds, they changed the bases, raked the dirt, and dashed back off the field.

"Wow!" Mike said. "If only I could clean my room that fast!"

When the game started again, the Blue Jays held on to their lead. As they took the field for the final inning, it looked as if they'd win. But the crowd grew quiet after the first three Mets batters loaded the bases with two outs.

When the next batter let two strikes go by, the Blue Jays fans relaxed a little. But the Mets

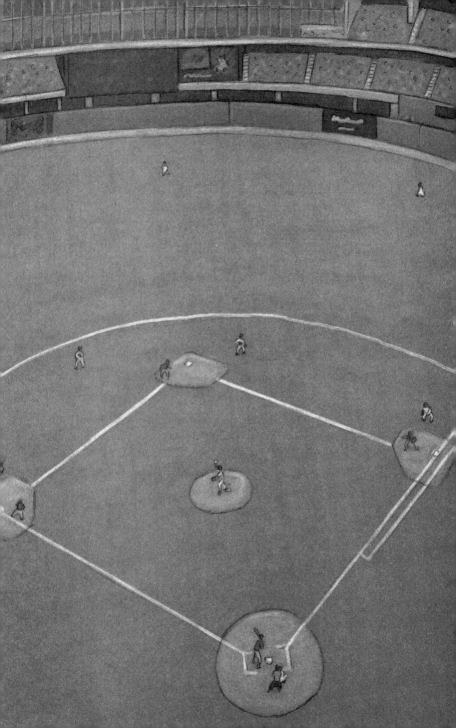

batter unwound on the next pitch and hit an easy ground ball to Dusty.

The ball rolled along the infield. Dusty scooped it up and then stood to throw to first. But when he opened his glove, it was empty.

He had missed the catch! The ball was still rolling for the outfield. Two Mets batters scored.

Dusty's streak was over!

# The Glowing Light

Mike and Kate shuffled slowly out of the stadium. Not only had the Blue Jays lost, but Dusty had made his first error!

Mike kicked a pebble out of his way. It bounced off the cement wall of the stadium. "Dusty won't win Rookie of the Year," he said.

Kate stuck her hands in her pockets. "It seemed like such an easy out," she said. "Something must be wrong with him. He almost missed that other play earlier in the game."

"Try not to worry too much," Mrs. Hopkins said. "One of the reporters said Dusty still has a chance of being named Rookie of the Year. He just needs to play well in the rest of the games."

"That's good," Mike said. "Maybe he'll play better tomorrow."

Mrs. Hopkins checked her watch. "It's almost dinnertime," she said. "How about we order room service tonight? You two can watch them clean up the ballpark while you're eating, and I can finish my story."

"Yippee!" Kate said. "That's a great idea!"

Mike perked up. "That sounds cool."

When they made it back to the room, Mike and Kate looked over the menu. Mike ordered a grilled cheese sandwich, while Kate ordered a chicken wrap. Then they settled down in two empty chairs near the window and watched as the last fans left the stadium. The bright lights were still on. A TV crew stood on the edge of the field, finishing up interviews.

It didn't take long for the room service to arrive. The waiter brought in a big tray and placed it on the desk. On the left side stood a stack of plates topped with shiny silver covers. On the right side were three tall glasses of milk. The silverware was bundled inside rolled-up cloth napkins. Mrs. Hopkins signed the bill and tipped the waiter. Meanwhile Mike and Kate took their dinners and sat in the comfy chairs in front of the window.

Even though Mike and Kate had been to plenty of baseball games, they'd never watched workers clean up a stadium after a game. Some of the workers had loud leaf blowers strapped to their backs. They walked down each aisle and blew clouds of napkins, hot dog wrappers, and empty popcorn boxes into piles at the end

of the rows. On the diamond, teams of workers tidied up home plate and the pitching mound. Another worker drove around the field in a special sweeper cart. The cart did one figure eight after another to smooth out the grass in the outfield.

By the time Mike and Kate had finished eating, most of the workers were done, too. The field was groomed for the next day's game, and the lights had been turned down. The baseball diamond was still lit, but most of the seats were not.

Mike and Kate returned their plates to the tray. Mrs. Hopkins was still working on her story at the desk.

Mike walked over to the window. He motioned for Kate to join him. Together they searched the bull pen for activity.

"Nothing there," Kate said. "It's probably still too early."

"It's not too early to plan for tonight," Mike whispered. "We can check again after your mom is asleep!"

"Good idea," Kate whispered.

Kate's mother finally finished working and offered to take them to the pool. They changed into their bathing suits and rode the elevator down to the lower level. Mike and Kate spent an hour splashing around and racing one another. Then the three of them played a game of tag in the pool.

Afterward, they each picked a different elevator and had an elevator race back to their floor. Mike thought he was going to win. Then someone got on his elevator to ride up one stop. Kate and Mrs. Hopkins popped out of their elevators at exactly the same time—it was a tie!

"Time for bed," Mrs. Hopkins said as they entered their room.

Mike and Kate put their pajamas on and brushed their teeth. Kate climbed into her bed and Mike slipped into his sleeping bag. Mrs. Hopkins let them read for fifteen minutes while she got ready for bed.

"We've got to get plenty of rest tonight," Mrs. Hopkins said. "Tomorrow's a big day. We're going to the Hockey Hall of Fame, and then we have a baseball game at night."

Mrs. Hopkins switched off the lamp. As soon as the light went out, Mike pretended to snore extra loudly until Kate tossed a pillow at him.

Mike sat straight up. "Hey!" he said. "I was sleeping. Couldn't you hear?"

Mrs. Hopkins switched the lamp back on.

Kate grabbed the pillow back. "The only thing I could hear was you pretending to be asleep!" she said.

Mrs. Hopkins clicked off the light. "Let's try this again," she said. "It's time for everyone to go to sleep."

This time, Mike and Kate rested quietly, waiting patiently for Mrs. Hopkins to fall asleep. It seemed to take forever, but after about thirty minutes, Kate hung her head over the side of the bed.

"I think she's asleep," Kate whispered to Mike, who was still curled up in his sleeping bag.

Kate had just started to climb out of bed when something caught her eye. Her jaw dropped open. She tapped Mike's shoulder and pointed to the corner of the room.

A blue light was glowing on the table!

# Slap Shot

"What is it?" Mike whispered. "Some kind of giant firefly?"

"Maybe it's a night-light," Kate whispered back. The soft blue light wasn't very bright, but it was definitely glowing.

Mike and Kate crept over to the table to find out what the blue light was. Once they got closer, they could easily tell.

It was the hockey puck they'd found at the game!

"I'd forgotten about this," Kate said. She

picked up the puck and looked at it closely.

"Me too," Mike said. "Where's the light coming from?"

Kate turned the puck over. There wasn't a lightbulb in the puck. It was simply glowing.

"You know what this looks like?" Kate asked. "Remember that Frisbee I got for my birthday? It glows in the dark. I charge it up under a light during the day and then I can see it at night. This must be a glow-in-the-dark hockey puck!"

Suddenly, Kate's mother rustled her bedcovers. Mike and Kate froze. Kate slipped the glowing hockey puck behind her back. They held their breath.

Kate's mother moved her pillow a little and turned over. She was still asleep.

Kate bent down and hid the glowing hockey puck under Mike's sleeping bag. Then she motioned for Mike to follow her as she crept over to the window. They pressed their noses up against the glass, but there were no lights in the bull pen tonight. They waited for a little while, but nothing happened.

Mike shifted from one foot to the other and almost lost his balance. As he caught himself, his elbow banged into the frame of the window.

He mouthed a silent "Ow!" to Kate and rubbed his elbow. But Kate shook her head. She put her finger to her lips and quietly opened the window.

Mike and Kate leaned out the window into the darkened stadium. The red EXIT lights glowed around the edges, but the field was dark. There was definitely no movement in the bull pen below them. Their sleuthing seemed like a bust again.

Kate was about to close the window when they heard something off to their left. It was soft but distinct.

*Swish . . . plunk.*

*Swish . . . plunk.*

Kate and Mike craned their necks to look all the way over to their left.

Flashes of blue streaked across the edge of the field.

"It's the lights!" Mike whispered. "Just like last night."

"They must be in the visitors' bull pen tonight," Kate whispered. "That's why we didn't see them until now."

Mike and Kate watched for a while. Then Kate nudged Mike. "Come on," she said. "I've got an idea." She closed the window slowly and then tiptoed across the room to the table near the hotel room door. Mike followed.

Kate picked up a flat key card from the table. She slipped the door open quietly. Mike pointed at her sleeping mother, but Kate shook her head. "It's okay," she whispered. "We'll be back in a minute."

Once they were outside the room, Kate closed the door carefully so it wouldn't make a loud *click*.

Mike and Kate stood in the hotel hallway in

their pajamas. All the other doors were closed. It was late, so everything was quiet.

"Are you crazy?" Mike asked. "What if your mother wakes up?"

"We won't be long," Kate said. "And she won't wake up. She's a heavy sleeper."

Mike looked around at the empty hallway and closed doors. "Okay, now what?" he asked.

"We just need to find a window that overlooks the visitors' bull pen," Kate said. "Then we can figure out what's going on. Maybe there's a window down there."

Kate ran softly to the far end of the hallway. But it dead-ended with nothing but doors on both sides.

Mike stared at the wall. "I've got an idea, too," he said. "It's *your* turn to follow *me*!"

Mike raced back down the hallway to the elevator. He hopped on with Kate when the elevator came a few seconds later. Mike pushed the button with *L* on it for the lobby.

"Maybe there's a window in the hallway on the far side of the lobby, near the soda machines," Mike said.

The elevator stopped. With a *bing!* the doors slid open, and Mike and Kate walked into the deserted hotel lobby. They had made it halfway across the lobby when a woman in a green uniform came out from behind the front desk. She raised one eyebrow at Kate and Mike.

"Can I help you?" she asked.

Mike and Kate stopped in their tracks. "Um, we were just thinking about looking for, um . . . ," Mike said.

The front desk clerk looked down her glasses at them. "Where are your parents?" she asked.

Kate stepped forward. She tugged on Mike's

baseball pajamas. "My cousin Mike just had a nightmare," she said. "He dreamt that the visitors' bull pen was filled with sharks. I was trying to show him it wasn't so he could get back to sleep."

The woman smiled and nodded. "I've had a lot of nightmares about the Blue Jays this season, but they've never involved sharks," she said. "I'm afraid there aren't really any windows that overlook the visitors' bull pen. But you might be able to catch a glimpse of it from the restaurant windows." She pointed to their right.

"Thanks," Kate said. She grabbed Mike's arm and pulled him toward the restaurant. "We'll take a quick peek and get right back to bed!"

Mike and Kate ducked through the open doors into the darkened restaurant. They ran to the floor-to-ceiling windows overlooking the field.

"Nice thinking back there," Mike said. "But maybe next time make the sharks man-eating. That's even scarier."

"The only thing scarier would be if *you* had actually thought of something smart back there," Kate said. "Why am *I* always the one to rescue us?"

"Because I'm the one always getting us into trouble," Mike said. "That's why we make a good pair!" He held up his hand and waited.

Kate rolled her eyes but still gave Mike a high five. "See anything?" she asked as she looked out the windows.

"Nope, this isn't any better," Mike said.

Kate thanked the front desk clerk on the way back to the elevator. Back on their floor, she opened the door to the hotel room quietly. Her mother was still asleep. Mike followed Kate across the room to the window. As they passed his sleeping bag, Mike accidentally kicked the hockey puck that Kate had hidden under it earlier. The puck flashed across the room in a bright blue blur and hit the curtain with a soft thud.

Kate grabbed Mike's arm. Her eyes were wide. "That's it!" she whispered. Kate slid the window open. They craned their heads and looked to the left. Listening closely, they could still hear the same sounds as before.

*Swish . . . plunk.*

*Swish . . . plunk.*

"You know what that is?" she asked.

"It's a ghost light," Mike said.

"No!" Kate said. "It's someone playing hockey! Someone's hitting glow-in-the-dark hockey pucks with a hockey stick in the bull pens!" She pointed to the visitors' bull pen on the other side of the outfield. "See? We hear the *swish* when the person hits the hockey puck with the stick. Then we see it light up as it goes flying. Then it goes *plunk* when it hits the end of the bull pen."

"I don't get it," Mike said. "There's no ice in

the bull pens. How could someone hit hockey pucks?"

"Easy," Kate said. "Don't you remember the time last year when we played street hockey? You don't really need ice to practice. Just some type of flat surface and a net to hit the puck into."

Mike and Kate listened to the sound of the hockey player and watched the blue streaks flash across the bull pen until suddenly the lights were gone and the stadium was dark.

# Time Travel

The next morning after breakfast, Mrs. Hopkins, Kate, and Mike walked a few blocks through Toronto's downtown to the Hockey Hall of Fame.

The hall of fame was in a fancy old stone bank building on a corner. Outside the building was a big metal sculpture of a group of kids leaning over an ice rink wall, waiting to play hockey. They wore helmets, big hockey gloves, and shoulder pads and held hockey sticks in their hands.

Mike ran behind the sculpture and draped his arm over the rink wall, as if he was waiting to take the ice, too. "Aunt Laura, take a picture of me," he called out.

Mrs. Hopkins took pictures of both Mike and Kate with the sculpture. Then they went into the hall of fame. Inside, it was a lot like the Baseball Hall of Fame back in Mike and Kate's hometown of Cooperstown. The museum was filled with exhibits of old equipment, information on famous players and teams, and videos of important hockey games.

Mrs. Hopkins let Mike and Kate explore the museum on their own. She made a plan to meet them at the entrance in a couple of hours, so they could walk back for the baseball game later that day.

Mike and Kate studied the floor map and took turns choosing what to look at. Mike really liked the replica of the dressing room for the Montreal Canadiens hockey team. He plopped down on one of the long red benches and pretended to lace up a pair of skates. "Come on,

Kate," he growled in a gruff voice. "Put on your skates and help me go out there and win the Stanley Cup!"

But Mike and Kate's favorite exhibit was a mini ice rink with a plastic floor. Visitors could use real hockey sticks to take shots with real hockey pucks against a computer-generated goalie. After waiting in line, Mike and Kate each got a turn. At first it looked like Mike was going to win, but Kate made her last three shots and tied with Mike.

As they were leaving the rink, Kate stopped in front of an exhibit with pictures of winning Stanley Cup teams. Mike pretended to skate back and forth down the hallway. After a while, he skated up to Kate and nudged her. "Come on, Kate," he said. "It's time to go."

But Kate didn't move. She was still in front of the wall filled with pictures of the winning

Stanley Cup teams. Kate was staring at one picture from thirty-five years ago.

"Take a look at this," she said. "It's impossible!"

Mike stood next to her. "Um, okay," he said. "You think they didn't have cameras back then? That doesn't seem that impossible to me."

Kate shook her head. "Don't be silly," she said. "Check out the hockey player in the middle of the front row. He's a time traveler!"

When Mike leaned in and took a close look, he let out a long, low whistle.

Right in the middle of the picture, standing behind the Stanley Cup, was a hockey player with bright blue eyes and curly hair. It was Dusty!

"Dusty is too young," Kate said. "He couldn't possibly have played on the Stanley Cup hockey team from thirty-five years ago!"

Mike studied the photo. The man standing behind the hockey cup looked exactly like Dusty. "I don't know," Mike said, shaking his head. "Maybe that explains why Dusty is nervous. He invented a time travel machine! If I did that, I'd use it to travel backward in time to play on all the great teams!"

Kate crossed her arms. "I'm not sure that's what's going on here." She stared at the picture some more. Below it was a plaque with the names of the hockey players. Kate looked for the names of the players in the first row. She read across the names. Smith, Allendale, Suraci, Martin, Timmons, Lesch.

Kate poked at the plaque with her finger. "That's it!" she said, her finger on the name Martin.

"See! I told you he was time-traveling!" Mike said. "How cool is that?"

"No, that's not it," Kate said. "The reason that man looks like Dusty is because it's Dusty's *father*! See, right here it says his name is Buck Martin. Dusty's last name is also Martin."

"You mean Buck? The guy who rescued my hat at batting practice and Niagara Falls?"

Mike asked. "But this guy has hair!" He pointed at the picture.

"Because he's thirty-five years older now," Kate said. "He's changed. But some things are still the same. He's still got blue eyes and that same chin. Dusty does, too."

Mike squinted. "I guess," he said. "So if Buck is Dusty's father, and he's a famous hockey player, maybe *he's* the one playing hockey at night!"

Kate shook her head. "He probably doesn't have access to the stadium," she said. "They'd only let in the players and workers. It can't be him."

"Maybe you're right," Mike said.

Kate stared at the photo of Dusty's father in his hockey equipment. "Hey, do you remember yesterday when we were waiting for Dusty in the clubhouse?" she asked. "He had all those pictures taped to the side of his locker."

Mike nodded. "Yeah, I remember," he said. "There were a lot of pictures of him playing baseball when he was younger."

"But he also had a lot of pictures of him playing *hockey*," Kate said. She tapped the picture again. "Think about it. Dusty has access to the stadium at night. He told us he's been up late because he's having trouble sleeping. He played hockey when he was little. And he has a really famous dad who played hockey. I'll bet *Dusty* is the one playing hockey at night!"

# A Confession

"Dusty?" Mike said. "But we asked him about the lights. He said he'd never seen them."

Kate smiled. "No, he didn't," she said. "He said he'd never seen anything in the stadium he couldn't explain. That's different from saying he'd never seen them. Of course he can explain the lights. Because he's the one out in the bull pen!"

"We've got to talk to him, then," Mike said. "Something fishy is going on. Let's find your mom."

Kate, Mike, and Mrs. Hopkins returned to the stadium just as batting practice was ending. Mrs. Hopkins headed off to the press room, while Mike and Kate ran down the aisle to the edge of the Blue Jays dugout. A few players were stretching nearby. Two workers in Blue Jays polo shirts were cleaning up. Mike and Kate waved until one of the workers came over.

Kate did the talking. "Can you please tell Dusty that his friends Mike and Kate need to talk to him?" she asked. "He told us we could ask for him."

"Sure," the worker said. He ducked into the Blue Jays dugout. Mike and Kate waited by the infield fence. They watched as the grounds crew painted the foul lines on the infield.

Finally, Dusty popped out of the dugout. "I don't have too long because I have to get ready for the game," he said. "What's up? Did you learn anything about the lights in the bull pen?"

"Kinda," Mike said. He scuffed the ground with his sneaker and glanced at Kate. "We think—"

"We think we figured it out," Kate said. "Someone's playing hockey in the bull pen at night."

"Really?" Dusty said. "But who would do that?"

"You!" Kate said. "We think you are playing hockey in the bull pen at night!"

Dusty's face lost its color. "What do you mean?" he asked.

"We just figured it out at the Hockey Hall of Fame," Mike said. "We saw the picture of your father winning the Stanley Cup. He looked exactly like you!"

"At first we thought *he* was the one playing

hockey," Kate added. "But then we realized he wouldn't have access to the stadium at night. But *you* would."

"Plus, you have all those pictures of you playing hockey in your locker," Mike said. "And you said you were up late at night. It had to be you. Why didn't you tell us yesterday?"

Dusty stood quietly for a moment. He was thinking. Then he glanced around to make sure no one was listening.

"Have you told anyone about this yet?" he asked.

"No," Mike said. "We wanted to talk to you first."

Dusty hung his head and smacked the palm of his glove a few times with his hand. "Well, you're right," he said. "I've been practicing hockey at night in the bull pen. I was trying to do it secretly, so people wouldn't know."

Just then, a Blue Jays player with a beard left the dugout. He noticed Dusty talking to Kate and Mike and gave a sharp whistle.

"Dusty! Coach wants to see you before the game!" the player shouted.

"Okay, I'll be there in a minute," Dusty answered. He turned to Mike and Kate and nodded. "I'm going to let you in on a secret," he said. "Make sure you stick around until the end of tonight's game."

"Why?" Mike asked. "What's going on?"

Dusty stared at the field for a minute, and then pounded his fist into his glove. "Because after tonight's game, I'm going to tell the press that I'm quitting baseball forever!" he said.

# Rookie of the Year

Mike's and Kate's jaws dropped open.

"What?" Kate asked.

"Are you crazy?" Mike asked. "You're up for Rookie of the Year! You can't quit!"

Dusty's shoulders slumped. "I have to!" he said. "I love baseball, but hockey's always been important to my family. I feel like I've let someone down by playing baseball. So I've decided to quit and play hockey instead."

Without another word, Dusty vanished into the clubhouse.

"Now what do we do?" Kate asked.

"He can't give up baseball!" Mike said. "He's got a shot at Rookie of the Year!"

"It sounds like he's made up his mind," Kate said.

Mike's eyes narrowed. "Or someone *else* has," he said. "Like his father. Dusty isn't quitting baseball because he doesn't like it. I'll bet he's quitting it because he feels guilty!"

Kate nodded. "We've got to stop him before he makes a huge mistake."

"Or maybe *his father* has to stop him," Mike said. "We need to find Buck before the end of the game." He bounded up the stairs and disappeared into the crowd.

Kate ran to catch up. She followed Mike to the section where they had seen Buck the day before, at batting practice. They walked up and down the aisles, looking for Buck. They

checked the seat that he had sat in earlier, but it was empty.

Mike and Kate were just about to head back when they spotted Buck. He was standing on the walkway behind the last row of seats.

When Buck saw Mike coming, he shook his head. "Oh no, I'm not going to have to rescue your hat again, am I?" he asked.

Mike laughed. "No, not this time," he said.

"But you're Dusty Martin's father, right? We saw your picture at the Hockey Hall of Fame."

Buck raised one eyebrow. "Yes . . . ," he said slowly. "Why?"

"That's what we thought," Kate said. "Dusty is about to make a big mistake! We need your help."

"What's going on?" Buck asked. "It sounds important."

"Dusty just told us he's going to give up baseball!" Kate said. "We think that *he thinks* you're disappointed in him. He's going to try to play hockey instead!"

"That's silly!" Buck said. "I'm sorry that Dusty didn't play hockey, but he's so great at baseball, he just can't give it up! As long as he enjoys it, I'll be happy."

"Can you meet us after the game?" Kate asked. "We'll go talk to Dusty before he talks to the press. You can tell him how you really feel. Maybe that will change his mind."

Buck nodded. "That's a good idea," he said. "I'll meet you near the dugout when the game's over. We can't let Dusty strike out at baseball!"

★ ★ ★

By the time Mike and Kate got back to their seats, the game was definitely going the Blue Jays' way. The Blue Jays had scored two runs in the first inning. Then they added on runs in the fifth and sixth innings to keep their lead.

Unlike the last few games, Dusty played really well. He hit back-to-back home runs and turned a double play to end an inning. He seemed on top of the world. When the game was over, he ran off the field to wild applause.

After the game, fans sang "O Canada" as they filed out. Mike and Kate made their way down to the Blue Jays dugout to meet up with

Buck, but he was nowhere in sight.

Kate checked the time. "Where is he? He's supposed to be here by now," she said.

"I don't know," Mike said. He continued to scan the aisles. Finally, he spotted Buck bounding down the stairs toward them.

"Sorry!" Buck said when he made it to Mike and Kate. "I got caught behind a big group of fans. Is there still time?"

"If we hurry," Kate said. "But we've got to run!"

They ran as fast as they could through the stadium to the team's media room. They were just about to open the media room door when a security guard stepped in front of it.

"Sorry, but only members of the press or the team are allowed in here," the guard said.

"But we've got something important to tell Dusty," Mike said.

The guard shook his head. "Sorry, but we can't let just anyone in," he said.

Buck stepped forward. He held out his driver's license for the guard to read. "We're not just anyone," he said. "I'm Dusty's father, and these are his friends Mike and Kate. Can you let us inside, please?"

The guard studied the license. Then he nodded and stepped aside. "That's good enough for
me," he said. "But be quiet, since the press con-
ference has already started."

Mike pulled the door open, and the three
rushed in. Dusty was just stepping up to the
microphone. Reporters swarmed around the

room, waiting for a big announcement. Men and women with video cameras lined the sides and back of the room.

Buck stopped short. Mike and Kate did, too.

"It's too late. I don't know if I should do this," Buck said. "This is Dusty's decision."

"But you've *got* to talk to him," Mike said. "He needs to know how you really feel."

Before Buck could answer, Dusty stepped forward and cleared his throat. He looked into the cameras. "Thank you for joining me here tonight. I've made a difficult decision that I want to share with all the Toronto Blue Jays fans," he said. "Playing baseball has been my lifelong dream. I'm lucky to have had a chance to play for the Blue Jays."

Dusty adjusted his baseball cap and took a deep breath. "I love baseball. But I also love my father, who first taught me how to play sports," he said. "He's the best athlete I know, and I want to make him proud. Hockey means everything to him. That's why I've made up my mind to—"

"Wait!" Mike called out from the back of the room. "You're making a huge mistake!"

All the reporters and video cameras in the room swiveled around to see what was going on.

Kate tugged on Buck's shirt. "Now's the time!" she said.

She and Mike pulled Buck through the crowd to the other side of the room. They emerged right in front of the podium.

Dusty's jaw dropped. "Dad, what are you doing here?" he asked.

"I'm here because I want to stop you from making the biggest mistake of your life," Buck said.

"What do you mean?" Dusty asked.

"Mike and Kate told me you had something important to say," Buck said. "But I have something important to say, too. You can't quit baseball. You're one of the best rookie players ever. You were born to play baseball."

"But I thought you wanted me to play hockey, like you," Dusty said. "I always thought that I was disappointing you by playing baseball. That's why I've been practicing hockey in secret at night. I've decided to quit baseball and play hockey instead."

"You can't do that," Buck said. "I'd love to see you play hockey like me, but I'm so proud of how well you're doing at baseball. You love baseball the way I love hockey."

"You're not disappointed in me?" Dusty asked.

"Not at all," Buck said. "I'm happy you found something that you love so much."

When he heard that, Dusty leaned over and
gave his father a big hug. *Click! Click! Click!*
All the reporters with cameras snapped away.
When Dusty and his father finally let go of

each other, someone handed Buck a hockey stick and Dusty his glove. The reporters took even more pictures.

After a few minutes, the reporters finished up and drifted away. Mike, Kate, Mrs. Hopkins, Buck, and Dusty were left alone. As the last reporter left the pressroom, Dusty snapped his fingers.

"I wonder if I should call them back in," Dusty said. "I just remembered there's one more thing I want to say."

"What's that?" Buck asked.

Dusty threw his arm around his father. "Well, thanks to Mike and Kate, I've got you back on my side," he said. "And that means that nothing is going to stop me from winning Rookie of the Year!"

# Dugout Notes
## ☆ Toronto ☆
## Blue Jays
## Ballpark

**Fast World Series winners.** The Toronto Blue Jays played their first game in 1977. They won their first World Series in 1992, just fifteen years later. The Blue Jays were the first team from outside the United States to win a World Series. And they came back the next year (1993) to win the World Series again!

99

**Stanley Cup.** The Stanley Cup is the tro-phy that's awarded to the best professional hockey team each year. It's named after Lord Stanley of Preston. He was governor general of Canada in the late 1880s. Lord Stanley first awarded the famous trophy in 1893.

**Hockey.** The first organized indoor hockey game was played in 1875 in Montreal, Canada. There are currently thirty National Hockey League teams, just as with baseball. But seven of the hockey teams are in Canada, compared with only one baseball team.

**Blue jays (the birds).** The blue jay is a songbird. Blue jays mostly blue, with some black and white feathers. They are smart birds that can be noisy and pushy. They like nuts and acorns. They live all over North America, from Florida up to Canada. Even though a blue jay's feathers look blue, they're actually dark-colored! The blue comes from the way light is reflected off the feathers.

**Blue Jays (the team).** The Toronto Blue Jays started in 1977. They were the second team outside the United States. The Montreal Expos (also in Canada) were the first. But the Montreal Expos became the Washington Nationals starting in 2005. Now the Blue Jays are the only team outside the United States.

**Two national anthems.** Before a Blue Jays game, fans have to stand for two national anthems! Since the Blue Jays are a Canadian team, "O Canada" is one. But since the Blue Jays always play an American team, "The Star-Spangled Banner" is the other. At home, the Canadian anthem is played last. On the road, the American anthem is played last.

**The Blue Jays' stadium.** The Blue Jays play inside a big stadium in downtown Toronto. When it opened, it was called the Sky Dome. The 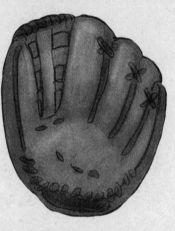 stadium's roof can be fully opened for games. The Blue Jays' stadium is the only ballpark with a hotel inside it.

Don't miss the next
Ballpark Mystery®!

# THE TIGER TROUBLES

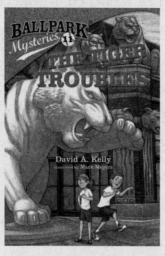

Someone has stolen a Detroit slugger's favorite baseball trophy! And unless he fills a tiger-shaped bag with signed baseballs, he'll never see the trophy again. Can Mike and Kate track down the thief?

# BATTER UP AND CRACK THE CASE!

## BASEBALL SLEUTHING FUN
## WITH MORE TO COME!

# Get ready for more baseball adventure!

Did Babe Ruth curse the Boston Red Sox
when he moved to the New York Yankees?

## Available now!